Withdrawn

W9-BXY-499

GRUMBLEBUNNY

BY **BOB HARTMAN**

ILLUSTRATED BY **DAVID CLARK**

G. P. PUTNAM'S SONS   NEW YORK

GLOUCESTER CITY LIBRARY

Text copyright © 2003 by Bob Hartman
Illustrations copyright © 2003 by David Clark
All rights reserved. This book, or parts thereof, may not be
reproduced in any form without permission in writing from the publisher,
G. P. PUTNAM'S SONS,
a division of Penguin Putnam Books for Young Readers,
345 Hudson Street, New York, NY 10014.
G. P. Putnam's Sons, Reg. U.S. Pat. & Tm. Off. Published simultaneously in Canada.
Manufactured in China by South China Printing Co. Ltd.
Designed by Gina DiMassi. Text set in Clichee.
The art was done in watercolors on Arches 140 hotpress paper.
Library of Congress Cataloging-in-Publication Data
Hartman, Bob.   Grumblebunny / by Bob Hartman ; illustrated by David Clark.
p. cm.   Summary: When three sweet rabbits and
one ill-tempered one encounter a hungry wolf,
they come to appreciate their differences in attitude.
[1. Attitude (Psychology)—Fiction. 2. Rabbits—Fiction. 3. Wolves—Fiction.]
I. Clark, David, ill. II. Title.   PZ7.H26723 Gr 2003   [E]—dc21   2001048251
ISBN 0-399-23780-1
1 3 5 7 9 10 8 6 4 2
First Impression

For Jon —B. H.

For ML, K, M & Betsy —D. C.

Once upon a time, in a Happy Hidey Hole, there lived the three sweetest rabbits on Misty Mountain Meadow—

Cuddlemop, Sweetsnuffle, and Pretty—

and their cousin Grumblebunny.

"What a lovely day it is!" said Cuddlemop one Misty Mountain morning.

"A perfectly lovely day, indeed!" agreed Sweetsnuffle.

"And what shall we do on this loveliest of most perfectly lovely days?" asked Pretty.

"It looks like rain," moaned Grumblebunny. "I say we go back to bed."

"Nonsense!" scolded Cuddlemop, in the nicest possible way. "Let's go and play with our friends the Beavers in their charming house by the Wide Water."

"Yes, indeed!" agreed Sweetsnuffle.

"The Beavers stink," groaned Grumblebunny. "And their house stinks. It's cold and damp and made of mud. I'm going back to bed."

"Come on, don't be a silly!" said Pretty.

So the three sweetest rabbits on Misty Mountain Meadow set off for the Beavers'. Along with their cousin Grumblebunny.

Soon they came to the Tall Tree Forest.

Cuddlemop looked up. "Ooh!" she said. "What tall, green trees."

"Ooh! Aah!" agreed Sweetsnuffle. "So very tall. And so very green."

"Ooh! Aah! Oomph!" cried Pretty, who looked up so high that she fell over backward.

But Grumblebunny was looking down at the ground. "Uh-oh," he said. "Those look just like the footprints of Bad Wolf Peter the Rabbit Eater. I knew we should have stayed in bed."

It was too late. The wolf was on them in a flash! And with a growl and a snarl and an evil laugh, he stuffed them into his snack sack, slung them over his shoulder, and carried them off to his Very Dark Cave.

"What a sturdy bag this is," noted Cuddlemop.
"A very sturdy bag, indeed!" agreed Sweetsnuffle.
"And what a nice, soft lining!" added Pretty.
"That's ME you're sitting on!" muttered Grumblebunny.

"GET OFF!"

When they got to the Very Dark Cave, Bad Wolf Peter the Rabbit Eater reached into his snack sack, pulled out the rabbits, and dumped them into a large pot of water on his stove.

"What warm, steamy water," said Cuddlemop.

"We never get water as warm or as steamy as this at home," agreed Sweetsnuffle.

Pretty climbed aboard a stick of celery. "This is the warmest, steamiest, toastiest, and loveliest water I have ever, ever, ever been in!"

Then she did a perfect Bunny Flop.

"This is not a bath!" growled Grumblebunny.

"WE'VE GOT TO GET OUT OF HERE!"

For the first time all day, Cuddlemop looked serious. She looked seriously at Sweetsnuffle, more seriously at Pretty, and most seriously of all at Grumblebunny.

"Grumblebunny," she said, "I have had enough of your grumbling. Can't you say anything nice about anyone?"

Just then, Bad Wolf Peter the Rabbit Eater scooped up some of the broth and slurped it with his slimy red tongue—up past his quivering lips, between his sharp yellow teeth, and into his dark cavern of a mouth.

Then he curled up his nose in disgust.
"Something has made my soup go sour!" he
growled. "It tastes bitter and nasty, and
it makes my belly feel all grumbly!"

Cuddlemop raised a paw to explain, but Grumblebunny spoke up first.

"YOU STUPID WOLF!" he hollered. "What did you expect? Don't you know that we are the four grumbliest rabbits on Misty Mountain Meadow? Any soup you make from us is bound to be horrible!"

Then Grumblebunny looked at the other rabbits and forced a little smile.

"It's a game," he whispered. "Just play along."

This seemed like a strange game to Cuddlemop, but she was pleased that Grumblebunny finally wanted to play. So she swallowed hard and said, in the grumbliest voice she could muster,

"THAT'S RIGHT, YOU VERY SILLY WOLF! We are the four grumbliest rabbits not only on Misty Mountain Meadow, but in the Tall Tree Forest as well. And any soup you make from us will be very horrible, indeed!"

"YES," agreed Sweetsnuffle, who was happy to play as well. "More horribly awful than any soup you have ever eaten!"

"Come, now." The wolf smiled. "There must be one cuddly, lovable, SWEET little bunny among you."

Then the wolf looked at Pretty. But Pretty loved games, too, and she was determined to be best of all.

"NO!" shouted Pretty at the top of her voice. "You great, ignorant, pea-brained excuse for a Rabbit Eater! We are the grumbliest grumbly creatures that have ever hopped or swum or flown or crawled in any meadow or forest or river anywhere in the world or the solar system or the universe! And any soup that is made from us will be so horribly, disgustingly awful that it will make the eyes explode and the tongue dry up and the teeth fall out and the belly burst of anyone who is stupid enough to eat it!"

The wolf had heard enough.
He picked up the pot,
carried it to the front door, and dumped
the contents onto the ground.

And the rabbits
raced back home.

When they reached their Happy Hidey Hole, the three sweet rabbits fell
to the ground, exhausted.

"What an exciting game!" huffed Cuddlemop.

"I couldn't agree more," puffed Sweetsnuffle. "A very exciting game, indeed!"

"The most thrilling and exciting game I have ever played!" added Pretty.
Then she looked at the others and smiled. "I've got an idea!" she said.
"Why don't we play with the wolf again tomorrow?"

But Grumblebunny said nothing.
He didn't complain or moan or even grumble one bit.

For he had already
gone back to bed.